I'm the Best!

Constanze von Kitzing

Barefoot Books
step inside a story

"I'm the **Loudest!**"
Said Little Lion.

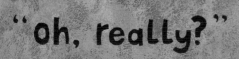
"oh, really?"

"What about me?"
roared Daddy Lion.

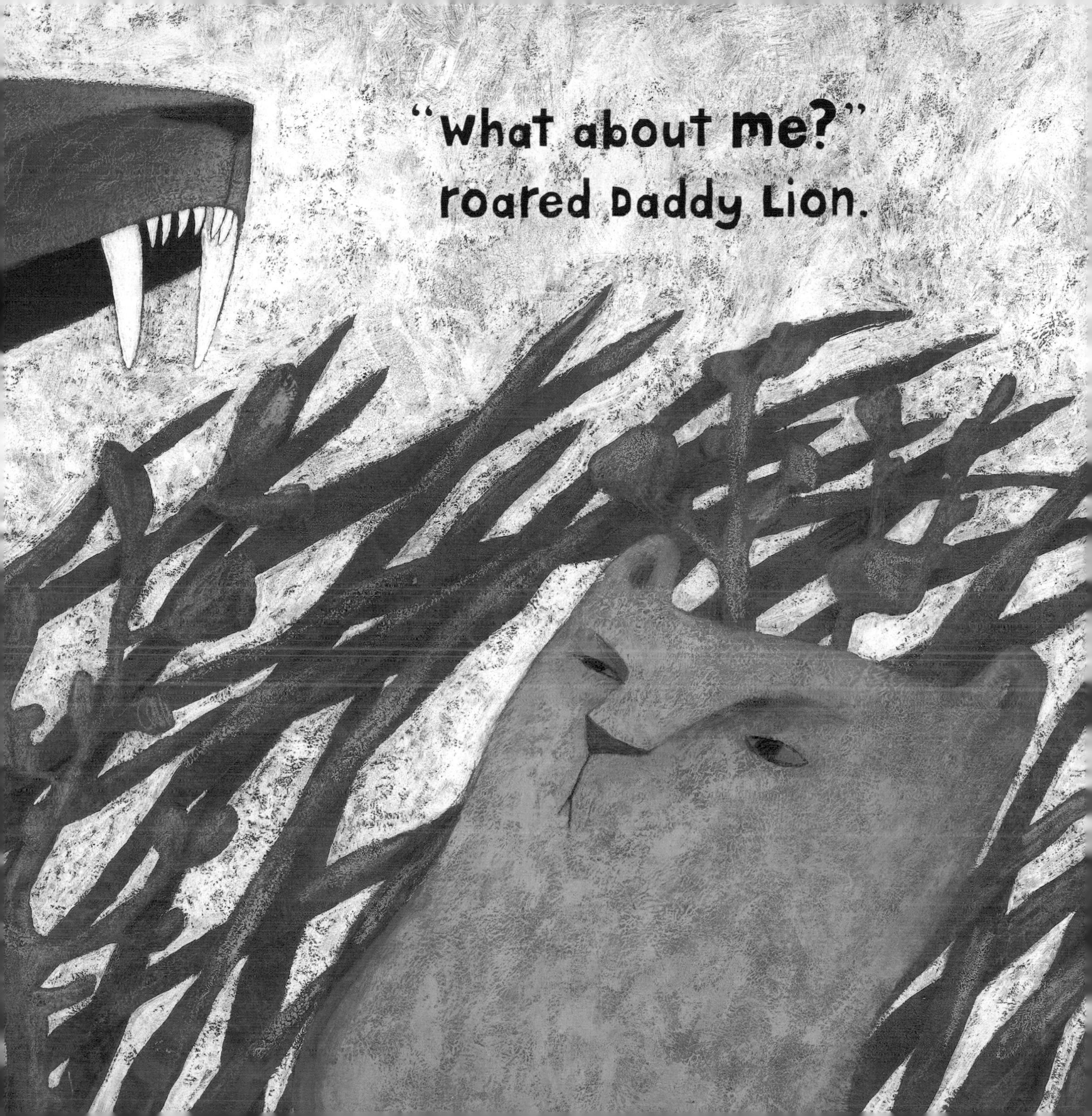

"I'm the **best climber!**"
Said Little Lion.

"Oh, really?"

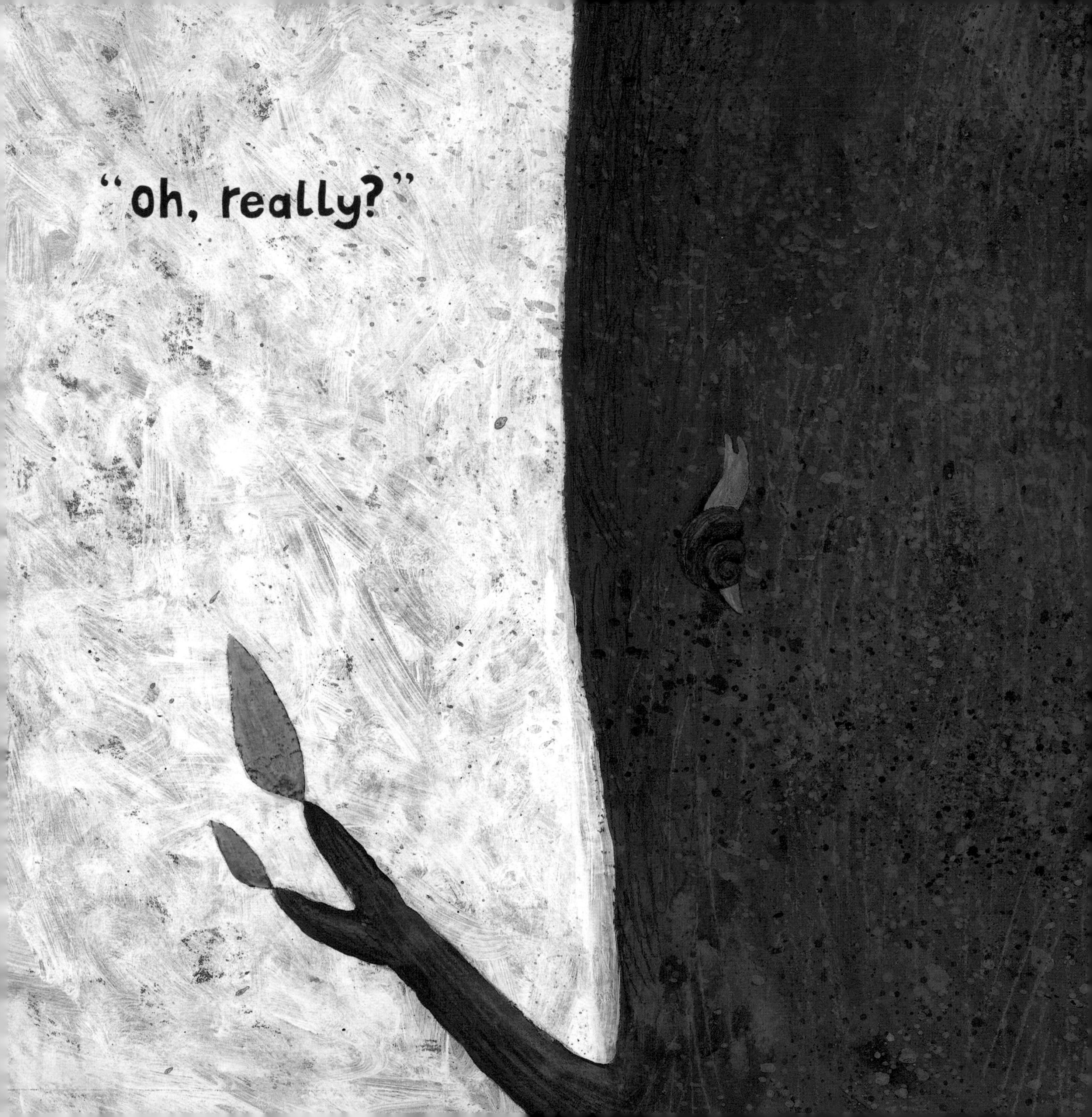

"What about **me**?"
grunted the ape.

"I'm the
fiercest!"
Said Little Lion.

"Oh, really?"

"what about me?" snapped the crocodile.

"I'm the **prettiest!**"
Said Little Lion.

"oh, really?"

"What about **me**?"
whispered the butterfly.

"To me,
    you're the **best**!"
   Said Little Brother.